For my own little tiger

First American edition published in 2019 by

CROCODILE BOOKS
An imprint of Interlink Publishing Group, Inc.
46 Crosby Street, Northampton, MA 01060
www.interlinkbooks.com

De tijger in mij
First published in Belgium and the Netherlands in 2018 by Clavis
Uitgeverij, Hasselt-Amsterdam-New York.

Text and illustrations copyright © Clavis Uitgeverij,
Hasselt-Amsterdam-New York, 2018, 2019

Library of Congress Cataloging-in-Publication data available:
ISBN-13: 978-1-62371-936-4

Printed and bound in Korea

Marieke van Ditshuizen

August the
TIGER

Crocodile Books, USA
An imprint of Interlink Publishing Group, Inc.
www.interlinkbooks.com

August is a **TIGER**, that's for sure,
because Mom always says he's WILD.
And tigers are WILD,
so August must be a **TIGER**.

"I'm a **TIGER**
and I scarf my food."
"August don't eat so WILD,"
says Mom.

"I'm a **TIGER** and I mark
my territory."
"August, don't pee so WILD!"

"I'm a **TIGER**, and I move SWIFTLY AND GRACEFULLY through the room."
"August, don't act so WILD!"

Mom puts August in the sandbox.
"This **TIGER** can also play outside," she says.

"I can't do anything," mumbles August.
"I wish I were a real **TIGER**,
then I would be really WILD."

"I am a **TIGER** and I dig a big hole."
"August!" yells Mom. "Calm down!"

Then August feels something strange. A deep growl rumbles
up from somewhere deep inside.

He wants to yell at his mom:
I'm a **TIGER**, and I don't calm down!
But when he opens his mouth, he hears ...

Did I do that? August even scares himself.
Then he looks at his body.
He's all hairy with beautiful stripes, with a long
tail to wave back and forth, and soft cushions under his paws.

He feels very strong!
He roars again: "WRAAAAAUWRRR!"

Then he jumps swiftly and gracefully over the hedge.
"August?" asks Mom, surprised.
But he can't hear her.

I'm a **TIGER** and
I can do whatever I like, he thinks.

Catch a zebra ...

Pee in public ...

Teach the neighbor's dog a lesson ...

Go to the jungle!

And with a wild jump, August the **TIGER** vanishes into the green.

I'm a **TIGER**
and I sneak through the
jungle in search of prey.

August reaches the playground in the park.

I'm a **TIGER**, and ...
Hey, there are my friends!
They'll be surprised!

August runs cheerfully to the playground.
"Hi! Can I play?"
But his friends don't recognize him.
They see a roaring **TIGER** running toward them.

The children are very scared and
they quickly **RUN** away.

August is all by himself.
"I just wanted to play," he grumbles softly.

Then his tiger ears catch the sound of
someone shouting far, far away.
"Auguuust! Where are you?"

MAMA!

August **ZOOMS** down the slide and he runs home as fast as he can.

Mom is in the doorway. "August?"

"Oh, what a relief! There you are!"
August leaps onto Mom.

They fall to the floor
together and they turn
SOMERSAULTS through
the room.

When their romp is over, Mom laughs.
"You're so big and strong!"

She strokes August's striped fur.
"And soft," she says.
"A little WILD, but soft."

August starts to snore.

"What was it like, being a **TIGER**?"
asks Mom when she puts August to bed.
"Nice. But my friends didn't want to play
with me," says August. He's a little sad.

"That's why I **DON'T** want to be a **TIGER** anymore, Mom."
"Tomorrow is another day, sweetie."
August is almost asleep.
"Tomorrow ..." he yawns ...

"Tomorrow I want to be a **DINOSAUR**!"